Alfie Gets in First

Published by The Trumpet Club
a division of Bantam Doubleday Dell Publishing Group, Inc.
666 Fifth Avenue, New York, New York 10103

Copyright © 1981 by Shirley Hughes

ISBN: 0-440-84128-3

Reprinted by arrangement with William Morrow & Company, Inc.
Printed in the United States of America
January 1990

10 9 8 7 6 5 4 3 2 1
UPC

Alfie Gets in First

Shirley Hughes

A TRUMPET CLUB SPECIAL EDITION

One day Alfie and Mom and Annie Rose were
coming home from shopping. Alfie ran on ahead
because he wanted to get home first. He ran
all the way from the corner to the front gate
and up the steps to the front door.

Then he sat down on the top step and waited
for the others. Along came Mom, pushing Annie
Rose and the groceries.

"I raced you!" called Alfie. "I'm back first,
so there!"

Annie Rose didn't care. She was tired. She sat
back in her stroller and sucked her thumb.

Mom put the brake on the stroller and left Annie Rose at the bottom of the steps while she lifted the basket of groceries up to the top. Then she found the key and opened the front door. Alfie dashed in ahead of her.

"I've won, I've won!" he shouted.

Mom put the basket down in the hall and went back down the steps to lift Annie Rose out of her stroller. But what do you think Alfie did then?

He gave the door a great big slam—BANG!
—just like that.

Then Mom was outside the door, holding
Annie Rose, and Alfie was inside with the
groceries. Mom's key was inside too.

"Open the door, Alfie," said Mom.

But Alfie didn't know how to open the door
from the inside. The catch was too high up.
Mom looked into the mail slot.

"Try to reach the catch and turn it," she said.
Alfie tried but he couldn't quite reach it.

"Can you put the key through the mail slot?"
asked Mom. But Alfie couldn't reach the
mail slot either.

Annie Rose was hungry as well as tired. She began to cry. Then Alfie began to cry too. He didn't like being all by himself on the other side of the door. Just then Mrs. MacNally came hurrying across the street to see what all the noise was about.

She and Mom said encouraging things into the mail slot.

But Alfie still couldn't open the door.

"Go and get your little chair from the living room and then you'll be able to reach the catch," said Mom. But Alfie didn't try to get his little chair. He just went on crying, louder and louder, and Annie Rose cried louder and louder too.

"There's my Maureen," said Mrs. MacNally. "I'm sure she'll be able to help."

Mrs. MacNally's Maureen was a big girl. Right away she came and joined Mom and Annie Rose and Mrs. MacNally on the top step.

"Mmm, might have to break a window," she said. "But I'll try to climb up the drainpipe first, if you like."

But Mrs. MacNally didn't like that idea at all.

"Oh no, Maureen, you might hurt yourself," she said.

Just then Alfie's very good friend the milkman came up the street in his milk truck.

When he saw Mom and Annie Rose and Mrs. MacNally
and Mrs. MacNally's Maureen all standing on the top
step, he stopped his truck and said, "What's the trouble?"
So they told him.
"Don't worry, mate," the milkman shouted. "We'll
soon have you out of there."

"Mmm, looks as though this lock's going to be difficult to break," said the milkman.

But then Mrs. MacNally's Maureen had a very good idea. She ran to ask the window cleaner, who was working up the street, if he would bring his ladder and climb up to the bathroom window. And, of course, when the window cleaner heard about Alfie, he came hurrying along with his ladder as quickly as he could.

Then Mom and Annie Rose and Mrs. MacNally and Mrs. MacNally's Maureen and the milkman all stood on the top step and watched while the window cleaner put his ladder up against the house. He started to climb up to the bathroom window. But when he was halfway up the ladder, what do you think happened?

The front door suddenly opened and there was Alfie! He had managed to reach the catch and turn it—like that—after all.

He was *very* pleased with himself.

He opened the front door as wide as it would go and stood back grandly to let everybody in.

Then the window cleaner came down from his
ladder, and he and the milkman and Mrs. MacNally's
Maureen and Mrs. MacNally and Annie Rose and Mom
and Alfie all went into the kitchen and had tea together.